Thanksgiving Reunion

Adaptation by Jamie White
Based on TV series teleplays
written by Ken Scarborough
Based on characters created by Susan Meddaugh

HOUGHTON MIFFLIN HARCOURT
Boston • New York

Daniel
Helen's dad
Mariela
Helen's mom
Jake
Helen's baby brother
Helen
Martha's best friend
Carolina
Helen's fashionable older cousin
Martha
the talking dog
Six
Mr. Felix
Caruso
Mom

Truman
Helen's smart and curious friend
Skits
the family's nontalking dog
T.D.
Helen's good and loyal friend
Alice
Helen's athletic but clumsy friend
Skipper
Cam
Mac
Sarge

ISBN: 978-0-547-86580-5 hc | ISBN: 978-0-547-86581-2 pa

Cover design by Rachel Newborn | Book design by Q2A Bill Smith Group

www.hmhbooks.com
www.marthathetalkingdog.com

Manufactured in China
SCP 10 9 8 7 6 5 4 3 2 1
4500420084

AN INVITATION FROM MARTHA

Gobble, gobble! Martha the talking dog here to tell you about my favorite holiday—Thanksgiving! We're talking scraps city. Leftover heaven. And more pie than Skits can shake a stick at.

But Thanksgiving is not just about eating. It's also about being thankful. For family. Friends. Turkey, gravy, sausage stuffing—oops! There I go again. I can't help it. I love eating almost as much as I love talking.

Ever since Helen fed me her alphabet soup, I've been able to speak . . . and speak . . . and speak. No one's sure how or why, but the letters in the soup traveled up to my brain instead of down to my stomach.

Now as long as I eat my daily bowl of alphabet soup, I can talk. To my family—Helen, baby Jake, Mom, Dad, and Skits, who only speaks Dog. To Helen's friends—T.D., Truman, and Alice. To anyone who'll listen.

Sometimes my family wishes I didn't talk *quite* so much, but they're thankful I can speak. One night I called 911 to stop a burglar! And saying "Please pass the peas!" sure beats begging.

This year's Turkey Day was full of surprises. Sit, stay, and hear all about it. You're invited to Martha's Thanksgiving!

COUSIN UCK

Mom had BIG plans for Thanksgiving. She sat by the phone, preparing to call a loooooong list of guests.

"Thanksgiving will be a family reunion," she said. "Our relatives are assembling from all over. Everyone is coming."

"Sounds like you'll need extra turkey, huh?" I hinted. "And extra gravy and—"

"We'll see, Martha."

I licked my chops. "I think we should have a reunion every day."

"Well, even if I could get it all organized and prepared, you couldn't have a reunion every day."

"Why not? I'm game."

"A reunion is when people get back together after a long time apart. You couldn't call it a reunion if you got together with your relatives every day," said Mom. "That's called a headache."

I ran outside to tell Helen the news. She was walking home from school with her cousin Carolina.

"So," said Carolina, "I told Tiffany 'prepare' means to get ready ahead of time. You can't spend three hours doing your hair, then try to prepare your project in class. I'm *never* doing a project with her again."

"Hey, guys!" I called. "Guess what? Guess what Mom's organizing? Guess!"

"What?" Helen asked.

"A FAMILY REUNION!"

The girls looked at each in horror.

"Oh no!" cried Carolina.

It turns out that family reunions can cause headaches even if they rarely happen. The girls sulked on Helen's bed.

Carolina groaned. "This is horrible!"

"What's the matter?" I asked. "This will be great. I can practically smell the gravy now."

"Uck," said Carolina.

"'Uck'? Seriously?" I said. "I'm sitting under your place at the table."

"She means Cousin Uck," said Helen. "His real name is Chuck. We just call him Uck."

"That's not very nice," I said. "You wouldn't like it if he called you Ick and Ack, would you? Or Ug and Erg. Or Guck and Gack!"

"Believe me," said Carolina. "It would be nothing compared to what Chuck does."

"Don't you remember the last family picnic a few years ago?" Helen asked.

Helen said it was going well until she sat with Carolina on a park bench . . .

"So," said Carolina. "I told Tiffany that 'organize' means to put things in neat order. You can't spend three hours organizing your purse, then try to organize your project two minutes before class. I'm *never* doing a project with her again."

Suddenly, Carolina looked up and gasped.

"What is it?" asked Helen. She hadn't noticed the messy boy who'd crept up behind her. With a sneaky grin, Cousin Uck dangled a worm over the back of Helen's shirt and dropped it.

"Eek!" she shrieked, leaping up. "What is it? WHAT IS IT? Agh!"

Uck laughed as she danced around, trying to shake out the worm. Helen shuddered at the memory.

"Maybe Uck is a good name after all," I agreed.

"I can't believe he's related to us," said Helen.

"I know what that's like," I said. "I had a brother who didn't seem like any of the rest of us."

"Who?" asked Helen.

"Number Eight. My youngest brother. He was kind of pushy."

"Eight?" asked Carolina. "That was his name?"

"With eight kids, Mom didn't have a lot of time to think up names," I said. "She called me Three. We all lived in this alley . . ."

Then it was my turn to tell a story.

ALWAYS USE YOUR BARK

I grew up on a dark, dirty alley. Restaurant trash cans overflowed with half-eaten food. The stench of rotting eggs and putrid meat filled the air. It was, in a word, *paradise*.

My whole family lived together. There was my oldest sister, One. She liked to bark at birds and paper.

Two and Seven always played together. You couldn't divide that pair.

Four loved to sing. Every time a horn honked, he let out a beautiful howl. *Owwww!*

Five liked to roll
in the mud.

The sixth one was
. . . Gosh, what was
her name? Oh, yeah.
Six. She was shy.

Eight wasn't shy, but
he didn't say much either.

Then there was me. I was
the eater of the family.

We had a happy life. But sometimes it could get a little scary. Trash trucks and delivery trucks rumbled through the alley at all hours. One night, my sister nearly got run over! Six was sitting in the middle of the alley when a truck sped right for her.

I ran and pushed her out of the way just in time. *Whoosh!* The truck zoomed past us and screeched to a halt.

Six hid as the driver stepped out, but I wasn't scared. I gave that lady a piece of my mind.

Ruff! Ruff! Ruff! Ruff! Ruff! Ruff!

"What have we here?" she asked, picking me up.

From the shadows came Mom's louder, more ferocious *RUFF! RUFF!* Nobody messed with her pups.

The driver peered into the darkness at my family. She must have really loved dogs, because as soon as she finished her delivery, she put all of us in the back of her truck and drove us out of the alley.

In the truck, my siblings happily ran around, barking at the sight of blue sky and sunshine. But I stayed curled up next to my mom. I was still shaky from what had happened.

Then Mom gave me the best advice: *Woof!* (That's "Always use your bark" in Dog.) Whenever something bad happens, a bark is a dog's best tool.

Soon the truck pulled up to the shelter.

This was the last day my family was together. Oh, how I missed them!

"Your mom would certainly be proud of you now, Martha," said Helen, patting my head.

I jumped off the bed and paced. "I wonder where she is," I said. "And my brothers and sisters."

"There's one way to find out," said Helen, smiling. "Invite them to Thanksgiving!"

"Great idea!" I said. "Could I?"

"Why not? You're part of the family," said Helen. "It would be fun to meet them. Check with Mom first. In the meantime, Carolina and I need to get ready. We have one week to prepare some anti-Uck strategies."

I raced downstairs to ask Mom.

"Dogs?" she said. "Why not?"

"Yay!" I cheered. "Come on, Skits! I'm going to find my family!"

KAZUO'S STORY

"I can't wait to trace my brothers and sisters," I told Skits as we walked to the shelter.

Woof? Skits barked.

"No, not 'trace' like drawing an outline around them," I replied. "'Trace' also means to search for something by following clues."

Woof!

"Exactly! Like tracing a cat to where it's hiding by that horrible cat smell. And I know just the person who can help me trace where my family has gone."

I found my friend Kazuo, the shelter's manager, inside. But when I asked about my family, he looked confused.

"But, Martha," he said, "you didn't come in with a family. You came here all by yourself."

"Huh? But that can't be," I said.

Skits and I followed Kazuo out to the yard, where he started raking some leaves.

"I'm telling you," I said. "I have a distinct memory of coming here with the rest of my family. At least, I'm pretty sure that I do."

Only now I wasn't so sure. Was my search over before it even began?

Kazuo leaned on his rake. "Well, dudette, all I can tell you is what I know. And I definitely remember finding you. I was in the Sheltermobile bringing in a stray . . ."

Kazuo had been driving along a country road, listening to his radio. (You should know he plays music loud enough to blow back a basset hound's ears.)

"YOU'RE IN MY MEMORY!" sang the rapper. *"A memory is when you think about something that happened. Like you might have a memory of a birthday party . . ."*

Kazuo almost didn't see the exhausted puppy on the side of the road. Me! As the Sheltermobile roared by, I fell to the ground.

"Whoa," Kazuo said, spotting me in his mirror. "What was THAT?"

He backed up to check out the sad lump of fur.

"Hey, pup! What's up?" Kazuo said, gently picking me up. "Are you okay, amiga?"

At the sound of his voice, my eyes flickered open.

"Then I took you back here," Kazuo said, wrapping up his story.

"But . . . could I have just imagined all that stuff about the alley and truck?" I asked.

"When I found you, you were pretty shaken up," said Kazuo. "I wouldn't be surprised if your memory wasn't that good."

A growly *WOOF!* came from the pound's back door. Kazuo's bulldog, Pops, stepped out.

"You DO?" I asked, amazed.

"What does he do?" asked Kazuo.

"Pops says he knows what happened!"

WHAT POPS SAW

WOOF! WOOF! barked Pops.

"He says you weren't working the day my family arrived," I translated for Kazuo. "Your cousin Kenji was."

Pops said that when my brothers and sisters arrived at the shelter, they playfully pounced all over Kenji. But one puppy hung back. Me. I wouldn't leave my mom's side.

The lady who rescued us thought it might be harder for an older dog like Mom to be adopted. And she could see that I didn't want to leave my mom, so she took us both.

"Do you need me to fill out any paperwork?" the lady asked Kenji.

"Nah," said Kenji. He was busy cuddling puppies and cooing, "So cute! Yes, you are."

"Did the lady say what her name was?" I asked Pops.

He shook his head.

I sighed. "I was afraid of that."

"Hang on," said Kazuo. "I might have something."

In his office, Kazuo looked through his files. "Kenji might not have been the most organized guy about doing the intake, but I would have recorded who adopted your brothers and sisters."

He pulled out a folder. "Here are the adoption forms from that time. We just have to figure out which of these puppies didn't have intake forms."

Soon Kazuo had seven adoption forms lined up on the counter. "That's them, all of your siblings."

"What about my mom?" I asked. "Do you know what happened to her?"

"No," said Kazuo. "But I have a feeling the answer could be staring us in the face."

"What do you mean?"

He held up the forms. "I mean that maybe one of your brothers or sisters knows what happened to your mom."

Kazuo's words filled me with hope.

"Then what are we waiting for?" I asked.

"Eeeeeeew!" Helen squealed. "Ew! Ew! EW!"

A slimy worm wiggled across the back of her hand.

"You can do it!" said Carolina, checking her stopwatch. "Just two seconds more."

At the kitchen table, they were practicing Anti-Uck Strategy #1: If presented with a worm, remain calm.

"OFF! OFF! TAKE IT OFF!" Helen shouted.

"Done!" said Carolina, dropping the worm into a coffee can. "You're doing great. If Uck tries anything, you'll be prepared."

I walked in as Helen ran to wash worm goo off her hand.

"Hey, Martha," said Carolina. "Any luck on your quest?"

"Yes!" I said. "Well, mostly. We traced all my brothers and sisters."

Kazuo, Pops, Skits, and I found my family all over town. We'd started with Two and Seven. They'd been adopted by a truck driver, who named them Cam and Mac. They drive all over the country. They say there isn't a state they haven't sniffed.

Next we traced Number Four, I mean, Caruso. He still sings, only now he howls duets with his owner, an opera singer.

Eight works as a guard dog in a factory. He's called Sarge now. He hasn't changed.

My brother Five has, though. We traced him to a groomer's. He wears a fancy collar and doesn't even mind being near cats! He says he's too grown up to roll in mud anymore. (I think he might be spending too much time with the cats.)

Six certainly came out of her shell. We found her eating a big plate of people food—while shooting a commercial! She's an actress. I hardly recognized her. She has the life, eating all day.

My oldest sister, One, works on a boat. She's called Skipper. She barks at birds to keep them away from the fish, and even has her own hat.

"Boy, all my siblings are doing really interesting things," I said to Skits as we walked back to the Sheltermobile. "I never get to do anything cool."

Woof!

"Firedog? Yes, I guess I did do that."

Woof! Woof! Woof! Woof! Woof! Woof! Woof!

"Sled dog, right. Radio announcer, telemarketer, sure. Teacher, spy, TV talk show host, head of a presidential task force . . . yeah, yeah. But, Skits," I cried, "I never once got to wear a hat!"

So that was it. I'd found all seven of my siblings.

"I arranged for them to come to Thanksgiving," I told Helen.

"It sounds like it all worked out," she replied.

"Except," I said, feeling that old sadness, "none of them knows where my mom is. I wish I had a memory of how I ended up out on that road. It's driving me crazy."

"Martha!" Dad called. "Phone!"

Who could it be? I wondered.

"Hello?" I answered.

"Hey, Martha!" said Kazuo. "I think one of these dogs wants to talk to you."

Woof! Woof, woof! Woof! Woof, woof! went the dogs.

"ONE AT A TIME!" Kazuo hollered in the background.

It was Cam and Mac! As I listened to their story, my heart thudded faster. "Uh-huh . . . uh-huh . . . WOW!"

The minute we hung up, I ran to the kitchen.
"What is it?" asked Helen.

They know where my mom is!

A GOOD EGG

The next morning, Kazuo drove us down the same road he'd found me on as a pup. As usual, the Sheltermobile's radio could be heard by every cow, dog, and chicken within miles. (I hoped they liked hip-hop.)

"I'M GOING ON A QUEST!" sang the rapper. *"When you go on a quest, you're looking long and hard for something. Like the way a knight might go on a quest to find a princess."*

Skits and I bopped along to the beat. Pops sat quietly in the back seat. He was having none of it

"THIS IS IT!" Kazuo shouted over the music.

"WHAT?" I asked, turning down the radio. Kazuo kept shouting anyway.

"This is where I found you!"

"Hey! That means Cam and Mac were right. The place where I lived must be right around here."

"I don't get how they know your mom lives around here," said Kazuo.

"They don't," I replied. "Not exactly. You see, that day in the alley, they noticed a large egg painted on the side of the lady's truck. Then, a couple years ago, they saw that same egg on a sign around here. They forgot about the connection until we reunited yesterday."

"Cool," said Kazuo.

"I'm going to see my mom again," I said, looking out the window. "I can't wait!"

"This is what I call a quest," he said.

On and on we drove. But we didn't see a single egg.

"You're sure this is the way?" Kazuo asked.

"It's just the way they described it," I said. "Smells the same and everything."

"We've come a long way from where I found you."

My ears drooped. "I know. But can we go just a little farther? It's got to be here."

We kept driving until the sun began to dip in the sky. *Come on, egg. Where are you, egg?* "Just

a little farther now," I said. "I know it's . . . LOOK!"

Painted on a sign in the distance was a big, white, beautiful egg.

TALKING DOG AT THE DOOR

"Hello?" called Kazuo. "Anybody here?

We waited by the door of a farmhouse. It didn't look like anybody was home. Skits stood up on his hind legs to peek into a window.

"See anything, Skits?" I asked.

Orow! he whined, hopping back down.

"Well, it looks sort of familiar," I said.

"Let's ask the neighbors," Kazuo suggested.

At the next house, a boy Helen's age and his dad answered the door. We asked if they knew the lady.

"Sure do. She's a chicken farmer," the man said. "Lived here quite a while."

"Where is she now?" asked Kazuo.

"Oh, she moved on a while back."

"Did she have a dog?" I asked breathlessly. "An older dog?"

The man looked surprised. "Yes, but . . . She didn't talk."

"THAT'S HER!" I shouted. "That's my mom!"

"I'll go look for her new address," said the man.

The boy waited with us. "You can *talk*?" he asked.

Do turkeys gobble? Do cats stink? I showed him my stuff. "Peter Piper picked a peck of pickled peppers," I replied.

The boy smiled.

"Hey," I said. "Do you remember a puppy who used to live next door?"

At this, the boy turned as white as a bone. He vanished into the house.

"That was weird," I said.

"Yeah," agreed Kazuo. "Was it something you said?"

The boy's father returned. "I looked through my papers," he said.

"And?" I asked.

"Don't have her new address."

I hung my head. "Oh."

"Got her name, though."

"You *do*? Great! What is it?"

"Smith. Mrs. Smith. Don't know where she is now. Different state, maybe."

Smith? I thought. There are a bazillion humans with the last name Smith. That's like searching the country for a dog named Max.

"Sir, do you remember anything else that might help us in our quest to trace her?" Kazuo asked.

"Not really," the man said. "That dog she had. I remember her. Funniest thing. Guess that old girl had a puppy that went missing."

My ears perked up.

"She'd go down to this rock and sit waiting for that puppy to come back," he recalled. "Went there every day, year in and year out."

I pictured my mom, all alone, waiting for me. I wondered when she'd stopped. Or if she was somewhere waiting for me like I'd been waiting for her. My eyes filled with tears.

Kazuo cleared his throat. "Well, um, thank you, sir. You've been a great help."

We rode home in the dark.

"I ran away?" I asked. "How could I do that to my mom?"

"I'm sure you wouldn't have done that," Kazuo said. "Something must have happened."

If only I could remember.

"Don't worry, Martha," said Kazuo as we pulled up to the house. "Pops and I will do everything we can to trace your mom."

"Thanks," I said, trying to sound cheerful. "If anybody can do it, you can."

But I felt lower than low. Not even the thought of Thanksgiving dinner could cheer me up.

33

THE RETURN OF UCK

Finally, the big day arrived. Thanksgiving Day! I was still sad about not finding my mom, but the smell of roasting turkey and a house full of loved ones can really lift a dog's spirits.

Most of my siblings had already arrived. We were still waiting for Five. (I crossed my paws that he wouldn't bring any of his cat friends.)

Cousin Uck hadn't come yet either.

Upstairs, Carolina dangled a worm in the air and cringed. "You sure you want to do this?" she asked.

"The only way to not be scared is to be prepared," said Helen. "And being prepared means getting ready ahead of time."

"But Helen, it's . . . it's . . ."

"Listen," said Helen, grabbing Carolina by the arms. "There's no choice. You've got to do it." She bravely turned around. "Worm me!"

"Okay," said Carolina. "You asked for it."

Helen's scream rang in every corner of our house and beyond.

AHHHHHHHHHHH!

In the backyard, my brothers and sisters barked (Except Four, who thought he'd heard singing and howled a lovely *OWWWWWWWWWWW!*)

In the middle of their duet, Five joined us.

"Five, you made it!" I said.

He barked, offended.

"Oh, right. I forgot," I said. "It's Mr. Felix now. I almost didn't recognize you."

Woof?

"*Recognize* means when you see someone or something and you know that you've known them before," I explained. "I didn't know who you were at first because I didn't recognize you without all the mud. Hey, speaking of mud, let me introduce you to Skits.

"*SKIIIIIIIIIIIIITS!*" I called.

But nobody came.

"I haven't seen him all day," I said. "Guess he's making plans to nab the turkey."

Meanwhile, Cousin Uck had finally arrived. Helen and Carolina spotted him through the window.

"Ready?" Carolina asked Helen.

"After seven days of having worms on me, I'm completely prepared for Uck," said Helen. "Nothing can be worse than that."

They crept downstairs, where Mom greeted Uck and his parents.

"Oh my goodness," she said. "Can this be Chuck? I hardly recognized you."

Helen and Carolina's jaws dropped. Cousin Uck wasn't messy at all. He didn't look like a boy who would touch a worm, much less drop one down anyone's shirt.

"A pleasure to see you again," he said to Mom. Then he walked past Helen and Carolina without a word. Or worm.

A moment later, the Sheltermobile pulled up in front of my house.

"Kazuo!" I cried. *He must have found her*, I thought. *Kazuo found my mom!*

HOMER'S STORY

Mommy, Mom, Mama! I thought, running outside to the Sheltermobile. *I was going to see my mom!*

"Did you find her, Kazuo?" I asked.

"No," he said.

My heart sank.

"But I found out what happened to you," he said, opening the door to reveal the boy from the farm. "Homer called because he had something he wanted to say."

"What is it?" I asked.

The boy looked at me shyly. "You saved me."

"Martha did?" asked Helen, joining us.

The boy nodded. "You remember that old fishing pier?" he asked me.

I shook my head.

"One day, I cut through your yard on my way to fish," Homer began. "I was eating a ham sandwich, and I think the smell of it made you follow me to the dock."

Okay, that part seems likely, I thought.

"It had rained a couple days before, so the river was high," he continued.

Homer's words triggered a memory. Of a rickety dock, tilting dangerously above the rushing water.

"That's right," I said. "My mom warned me to stay away from that old pier. I tried to stop you!"

Ruff, ruff, ruff! I'd barked, nipping at Homer's ankle. But he shook me off and kept walking. I ran ahead onto the dock, blocking his path before he could step onto it.

RUFF, RUFF, RUFF, RUFF!

I used my bark. Just like Mom had taught me to do. Homer jumped back, surprised. Suddenly, there was a loud creak, and the dock below my paws broke away with a *SNAP!*. I was swept downstream.

Ruff! Ruff! Ruff! I cried.

I was so frightened. Homer looked scared too. He dropped his fishing pole and ran after me along the riverbank, but the current was too fast. I watched him grow smaller and smaller and then disappear.

It was a bumpy ride. I held on tight. But then a huge rock rose in the middle of the river. It got closer. And CLOSER. My raft crashed into it. I fell into the water.

Splash!

I paddled to the bank and fell into a heap. I knew I had to get back up. My mom would be worried. So I dragged myself out of the woods to the road, thinking of home. But I was so dog-tired, I collapsed.

When I came to, a scruffy-looking guy was standing over me. "Hey, pup! What's up?" he asked.

Finally, I'd uncovered my past.

Kazuo traced my long route along a map spread out on the sidewalk. "So that's how you got from here all the way down here."

"I'm sorry," said Homer. "I was afraid to tell. Especially when I saw your mom looking for you. I didn't even know you made it till the other day."

"Thanks for telling me," I said. "That was brave."

"I guess I won't see my mom again after all," I said to Helen after Kazuo left. "I'll only have memories of her. Like how, before my eyes opened, she was just a nice warm tongue.

"And how she always shifted around to make room for me at dinner," I added, thinking of me squeezing in with my brothers and sisters.

"And there was this one time when a big raccoon came into the alley and Mom scared it away with her bark," I said. "She made me feel safe."

"And I guess I'm mostly sad that she thinks I ran away and didn't want to be with her anymore."

Helen put her arm around me. "I'm sure your mom didn't think that, Martha. She knew you too well."

We sat on the porch in silence when a van with a familiar-looking passenger pulled up in front of us.

"Skits?" said Helen.

The driver came out to greet us. "Craziest thing," he said. "He was standing at my boss's doorway, barking and howling. He's yours, though?"

"Yes," said Helen.

The man opened the door and Skits hopped out.

"Skits!" Helen exclaimed. "What were you doing?"

Woof!

"WHAT?" I asked. "Where?"

I turned to the van to see an older dog looking at me kindly. A warm feeling spread from the tips of my ears to the bottom of my paws.

"MOM!" I cried. "Mom! Mommy!"

She was older now, but it was her, all right. Just as I'd dreamed. She even smelled the same. I jumped all around in excitement, barking woofs of endearment.

"They found you! You're back," I sighed, nuzzling up against her soft fur. "I missed you soooo much!"

I didn't leave my mom's side all day. We had lots to catch up on. I told her all about my life, and gave her a tour of my home.

First I showed her my room. "Well, mine and Helen's," I said.

Then I showed her my bowl. “This is where my alphabet soup goes!”

And the phone. “This is how I order pizza.”

Mom hung her head and sadly walked away.

“Mom?” I said, going to her side. “What’s the matter?”

Woof?

“The other puppies?” I repeated. “You mean my brothers and sisters?”

Mom nodded slowly.

“Actually,” I said, “I think I have an idea what happened to them.”

HAPPY THANKSGIVING!

"Mom," I said. "Brace yourself."

At the sight of all her pups reunited, Mom's mouth opened in surprise. A silent tear ran down her jowls.

Everyone ran forward and covered her in slobbery kisses.

I hung back with Skits and Helen, to watch. "I thought I'd *never* see her again."

"How did you find her, Skits?" Helen asked.

Skits said he had an idea. He snuck out early that morning on a quest. He didn't tell me because he didn't want me to get my hopes up. He went back to the alley, where he waited for a certain truck to come along. Mrs. Smith's delivery truck!

When it stopped, Skits hopped into the back and hid. And when the truck pulled into Mrs. Smith's new farm, Skits saw my mom. He leaped out of the truck to tell her about me.

While Mrs. Smith and her deliveryman read Skits's address on his tags, Mom slipped into the truck.

"I guess she wants to go too," said Mrs. Smith.

And that's what she did.

"Skits, you're a genius!" said Helen.

"DINNER!" Dad called.

My brothers and sisters raced to claim their spots under the kids' table.

It was the best and biggest Thanksgiving ever. Everybody was there—friends and family, new and old. Even Mrs. Smith came. I curled up cozily on my chair with my mom.

"Let's hear it for our hostess!" a guest toasted. We all cheered for Mom . . .

Well, except for Chuck. He didn't look happy to be sitting at the kids' table.

Carolina was telling him a story. "I told her you can't assemble an entire Conestoga wagon model on the day it's due. I'm so *never* going to do a project with Tiffany again."

Chuck crinkled his nose in disgust. "Why are all these dogs under the table?" he asked.

"Oh, we always have that," said Helen. "It's called the dogs' table."

"Happy Thanksgiving!" I said, giving Helen a kiss.

"Happy Thanksgiving, Martha!" she said.

"I'm the luckiest one here," I said. "I have *two* families!"

But there was still one thing missing. "Now," I said, "about that turkey . . ."

GLOSSARY

How many words do you remember from the story?

arrange: to put things in a neat order or to plan for something

assemble: to bring together

connection: a link shared with another person

memory: when you think about something that happened to you

organize: to put things in a neat order

prepare: to get ready ahead of time

quest: a long and difficult search for something

recognize: to see someone or something and know that you've seen them before

reunion: when people get back together after a long time apart

trace: to search for someone or something by following clues

AROUND THE TABLE

Martha's family loves to play games at the dinner table, especially on Thanksgiving. Try out some of her favorites!

PASS THE TURKEY

Draw a turkey's face on the rubber end of a badminton shuttlecock. Then "pass the turkey" to one of your dinner guests. As each person catches it, he names what he's thankful for, starting with the letter A. Then he tosses it to another player, who will use the letter B, and so on. For example, for L, Martha says, "I'm thankful for leftovers."

As a variation, guests can share their favorite memories of the year.

SILLY SUPPER

Start a silly story, and let each person take turns adding to it. Try to reach its conclusion by the time dinner ends. Players get one point for each word they use from the glossary, and two points for making somebody laugh. The one with the most points by dessert wins!

DREAM REUNION

Pretend you're organizing a reunion and can reconnect with *anyone* you'd like—friends, family, celebrities, athletes, or even historical figures. Ask each person at the dinner table who they'd reunite with and why.